The Zachary's Plans

Written by Jill Eggleton
Illustrated by Kelvin Hawley

Rigby

Mr. and Mrs. Zachary were building a new house.

> *I want a house with a big living room. I need a living room to relax in with my swinging chair, my books, my exercycle, and my drums.*

So Mr. Zachary drew a plan to show Mrs. Zachary.

Description:
The house is shaped like a large M. It is made from yellow bricks. Inside, the house has six rooms. The living room is the biggest room. It has a swinging chair in one corner and in the middle of the room there is a platform for drums. The platform hangs from the ceiling by chains. There is a ladder for getting up and down. The inside walls are green and yellow.

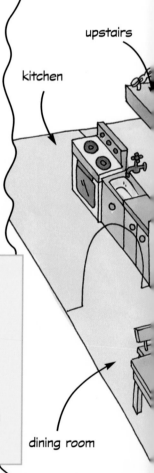

upstairs

kitchen

dining room

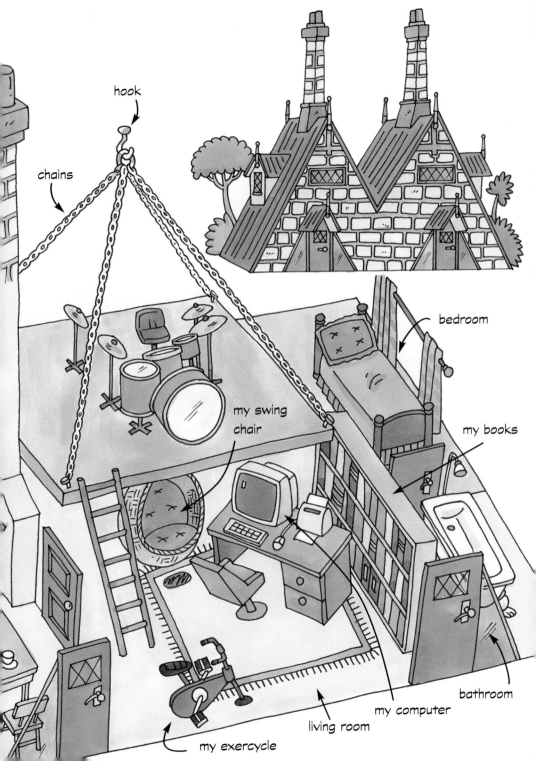

hook

chains

bedroom

my swing
chair

my books

my computer

living room

my exercycle

bathroom

Mrs. Zachary looked at Mr. Zachary's plan, but she didn't like it.

> *The living room is not the most important room in a house. The bathroom is. I want a huge bathroom with a bathtub the size of a swimming pool. I want a slide and a diving board. I want a soaping machine and a drying fan.*

So Mrs. Zachary drew a plan to show Mr. Zachary.

dining room

kitchen

living room

Description:
The house is oblong. The outside walls are made of stone. Inside, the house has ten rooms. The bathroom is the biggest room. It has a bathtub as large as a swimming pool with a slide and a diving board. There is a soaping machine and a drying fan.

diving board

soaping machine

drying fan

spa

slide

bedroom

Mr. Z's
bathroom

But Mr. Zachary didn't like Mrs. Zachary's plan. He went to talk to the neighbor.

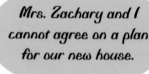

Mrs. Zachary and I cannot agree on a plan for our new house.

laundry room

The next day, the neighbor came over with a new plan.

Description:
The house is long and looks like an old bus. It has a row of small windows on each side and windows in the roof. The outside is made of tin. Inside, the house has six rooms. The dining room is the biggest. It has a huge, long table with short legs. In the middle of the table is a train track. The train carries the food around the table. The colors inside the house are very bright. Every room is a different color.

kitchen

bunks

rmchairs

dining room table

bathroom

Mrs. Zachary didn't like the neighbor's plan. She talked to her hairdresser about the problems with the new house.

Mr. Zachary and I cannot agree on a plan for our new house.

The hairdresser drew a plan on a paper towel and showed it to Mrs. Zachary.

Description:
The house is round with round windows and doors. It is made of baked mud. Inside, the house has four rooms. The biggest room is the laundry room. The laundry room has two washing machines and big fans. In one corner, there is a bed for sleeping when there is a lot of wash to be done.

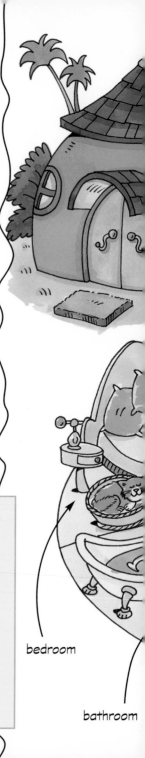

bedroom

bathroom

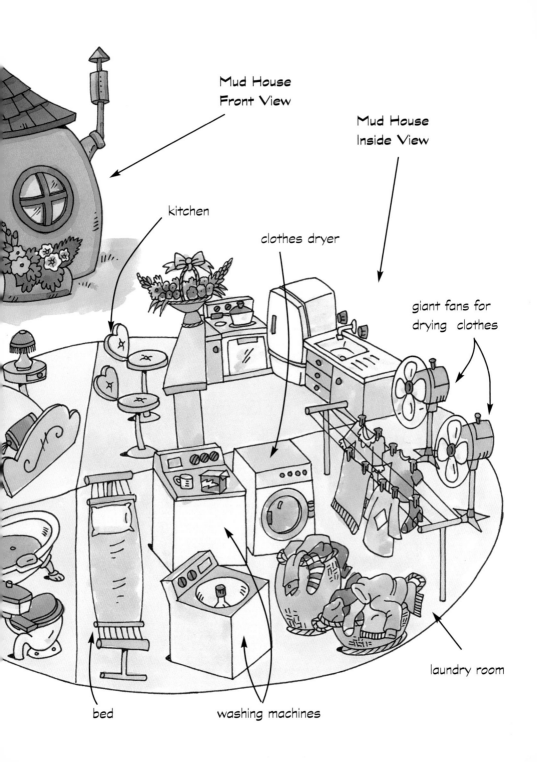

Mud House
Front View

Mud House
Inside View

kitchen

clothes dryer

giant fans for
drying clothes

bed

washing machines

laundry room

Mr. Zachary looked at the hairdresser's plan. "Too fussy!" he said. He talked to his bus driver on his way to work.

Mrs. Zachary and I just cannot agree on a plan for our new house.

The bus driver drew a plan on a ticket stub.

Description:
The house has several different shapes. The walls of the house are made of wood and the roof is made of tin. Inside, the house has two rooms. The biggest one is the bedroom. The bedroom has furniture that rolls out from the wall when it is needed. The color of the house is purple and green.

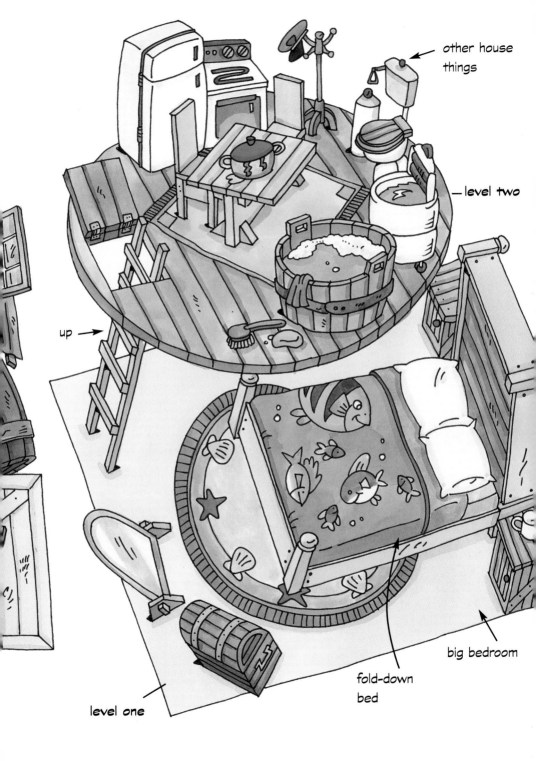

other house
things

— level two

up →

big bedroom

fold-down
bed

level one

Mrs. Zachary looked at the plan. "That's no good!" she said. She told her dentist about the house troubles.

Mr. Zachary and I are having big problems. We cannot agree on a plan for our new house.

The dentist drew a plan on a paper bib.

dining room

Description:

The house has two levels. The outside is made of white stone. The windows and doors are wooden and painted bright red. Inside, the house has eight rooms. The biggest room is the kitchen. Along one wall of the kitchen there are built-in gadgets. On the other wall there is a row of stoves. The dishwasher is built into one end. It is big enough to hold two weeks worth of dirty dishes. The color of the house inside is purple and yellow, except for the doors.

lots of stoves

edroom

spa

bathroom

laundry room

spare room

kitchen

dishwasher

The Zacharys looked at the dentist's plan. "Too small!" they said.

Finally, Mrs. Zachary had an idea.

You can plan half the house, and I will plan half the house. We will join it with a tunnel.

Great!

dining room

fan

Description of the Tunnel:
The top and the sides of the tunnel are made of green glass. The floor is made of thick rubber.
In the center of the tunnel are two large chairs that fold down into beds. There is a coffee machine and a stereo. These are operated by remote controls on the swivel chairs. By the glass wall on one side of the tunnel, there are little stands for candles.

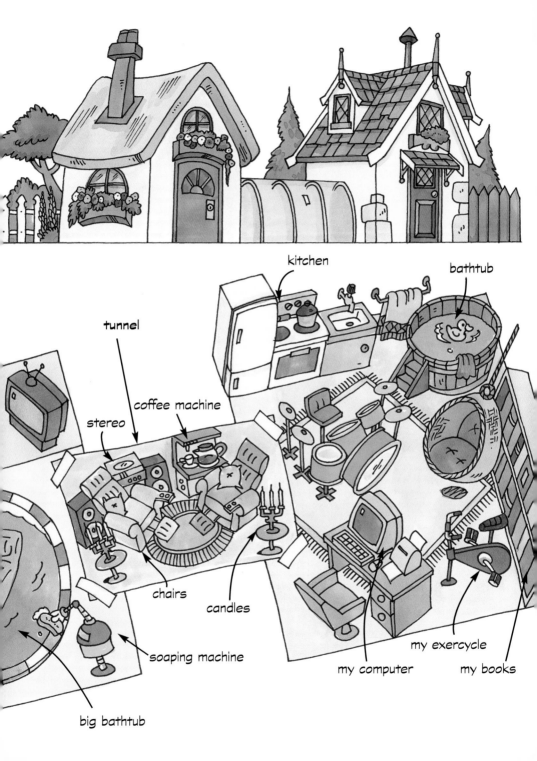

kitchen

bathtub

tunnel

coffee machine

stereo

chairs

candles

soaping machine

my exercycle

my computer

my books

big bathtub

At last the Zacharys have their new house. The thing they like the best in the house is the tunnel. They sit in the tunnel and talk and talk. Sometimes they sing, and their voices bounce off the walls and float through the town.

Description – Plan

Descriptions are like talking pictures. You can write descriptions about characters, events, places, and things. The people in my book have written descriptions about their house plans.

How to write descriptions for house plans:

Step One

Draw a plan of your house, or a house you would like to live in. To help you draw the inside of your house, imagine that you are on the ceiling. Show just the top of things in your house. You can label your plan.

Step Two
Now use your plan to write down all the things you can about your house.

○ Use words that describe:
  - shape
  - size
  - color
  - textures
  - things inside the house

○ Use words that describe where things are placed:
  - up
  - above
  - level one
  - below

Step Three
Check your description. Can you add anything to it? Is your description like a talking picture?

■■■■ Guide Notes

Title: The Zacharys' Plans
Stage: Fluency (2)

Text Form: Description – Plan
Approach: Guided Reading
Processes: Thinking Critically, Exploring Language, Processing Information
Written and Visual Focus: Plan Description, Speech Bubbles, Labels

THINKING CRITICALLY
(sample questions)
- Why do you think Mr. Zachary wanted a platform for his drums?
- Why do you think Mrs. Zachary wanted the bathroom to be the biggest room?
- Why do you think it was necessary to have a train track on the table?
- Which house would you prefer to live in? Why?

EXPLORING LANGUAGE

Terminology
Spread, author and illustrator credits, ISBN number

Vocabulary
Clarify: bib, platform, fussy, gadgets, dome
Nouns: plan, house, bathroom
Verbs: draw, talk, carry, sleep
Singular/plural: drum/drums, room/rooms, door/doors

Print Conventions
Apostrophes – possessive (The Zacharys' Plans, hairdresser's plans),
contraction (didn't)

Phonological Patterns
Focus on short and long vowel **a** (ladder, plan, track, label, came)
Discuss root words – biggest, swimming, diving, carries
Look at suffix **ly** (absolutely), **y** (fussy, dirty)